For Jack

Ω

Published by
PEACHTREE PUBLISHERS, LTD.
1700 Chattahoochee Avenue
Atlanta, Georgia 30318-2112
www.peachtree-online.com

ISBN 1-56145-298-X

Text and Illustration © 2003 by John Butler
First published by Orchard Books in Great Britain, 2003

10 9 8 7 6 5 4 3 2 1
Printed in Singapore

Library of Congress Cataloging-in-Publication Data:
Butler, John.
  Cuddle like a koala / written and illustrated by John Butler -- 1st
ed.
      p. cm.
Summary: Rhyming text describes how various animals move.
  ISBN 1-56145-298-X
  [1. Animals--Fiction. 2. Stories in rhyme.] I. Title.
  PZ8.3.B9785 Cu 2003
  [E]--dc21   2003004334

Can You Cuddle Like a Koala?

John Butler

PEACHTREE
ATLANTA

Pretend you're an animal.

What can you be?

Can you copy these creatures?

Are you ready?

Let's see.

Can you **cuddle**
like a koala and
hold on tight?

Can you **creep** like a mouse

in the pale moonlight?

Can you swing

like a monkey, wild and free?

Can you **wink**
like an owl and hide
in a tree?

Can you

leap like a frog
in a cold, clear stream?

Can you S t r e t c h

like a tiger, waking from a dream?

Can you

splash

like an otter

in the pond so deep?

Can you jump like a hare,

with a hop and a leap?

Can you hug
like a bear
with all your might?

Can you **curl up** like a squirrel getting ready for the night?

Now copy these creatures, all ready for bed.

Close your eyes tight and rest your sleepy head.